Suncatcher

JOSE PIMIENTA

Also by Jose Pimienta
Soupy Leaves Home
The Leg

....

Cover art, text, and interior illustrations copyright © 2020 by Jose Pimienta

All rights reserved. Published in the United States by RH Graphic,
an imprint of Random House Children's Books, a division of Penguin Random House LLC, New York.
Originally published through Kickstarter in 2019.

RH Graphic with the book design is a trademark of Penguin Random House LLC.

Visit us on the Web! RHKidsGraphic.com • @RHKidsGraphic

Educators and librarians, for a variety of teaching tools, visit us at RHTeachersLibrarians.com

Library of Congress Cataloging-in-Publication Data
Name: Pimienta, Jose, author, artist.
Title: Suncatcher / Jose Pimienta.
Description: First RH Graphic edition. | New York : RH Graphic, [2020] | Audience: Ages 14–18 | Audience: Grades 10–12 | Summary: "Beatriz must play the perfect song in order to free her grandfather's soul from his guitar after he passes away"—Provided by publisher.
Identifiers: LCCN 2019026149 | ISBN 978-0-593-12481-9 (paperback) | ISBN 978-0-593-12482-6 (hardcover) ISBN 978-0-593-12525-0 (library binding) | ISBN 978-0-593-12483-3 (ebook)
Subjects: LCSH: Graphic novels. | CYAC: Graphic novels. | Music—Fiction. |
Death—Fiction. | Grandfathers—Fiction.
Classification: LCC PZ7.7.P5316 Sun 2020 | DDC 741.5/973—dc23

Designed by Patrick Crotty

MANUFACTURED IN CHINA
10 9 8 7 6 5 4 3 2 1
First RH Graphic Edition

A comic on every bookshelf.

FOR THE MEXICALI BANDS
AND THEIR FANS

To me, the best songs are the ones that I can listen to with my headphones on and drift into dreams with.

When I'm under the rhythms of my heroes—

—I am at home.

3

4

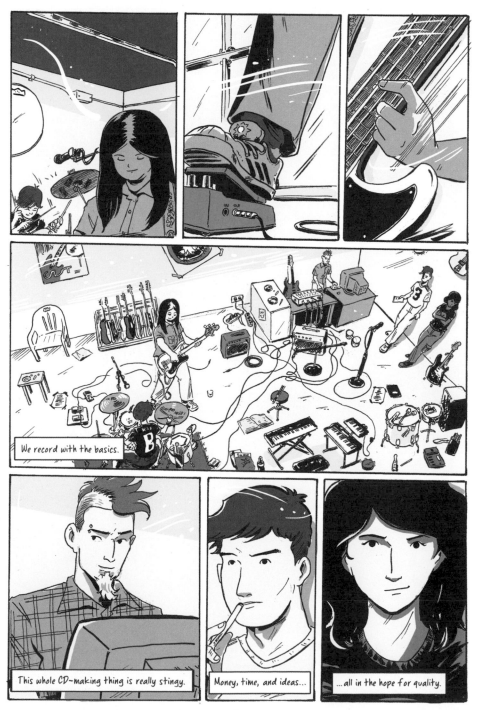

We record with the basics.

This whole CD-making thing is really stingy.

Money, time, and ideas...

...all in the hope for quality.

These demos are costing us quite the penny—

—considering we're doing it ourselves.

But the one song under my sleeve—

—is going to be worth every bar of it.

9

10

11

14

15

16

JULY 1997

My parents cried when Tata passed.

I didn't.

I felt something else.

20

21

On that same trip, when I got to Sinaloa, by the coast of Mazatlán, I met her. My lovely Tencha.

Not long later, I married and I took a different route than my youthful dreams.

Mario & Tencha

I set the guitar aside and raised a family.

My head was clearer and clearer every day. But that one killer song remained wanting to be played.

The weight made me ill and took me slowly.

I never used the skills he gave me, but that was not his concern. When he came to collect, I tried one more bargain.

WE ARE THE YOUTH IN THE YEAR 2000

I've been in a few bands. In this punk-ska, the singer's rants are a positive energy, but... I'm not a good fit.

I wanna make music for something important. These guys are just making jokes.

Rehearsals are a total waste of time, and we're lousy at gigs.

I'm starting to think I'll never find a band to help me finish.

41

44

45

47

48

49

50

51

52

54

55

PUNK ROCK, MI VIDA ESTÁ BIEN.

57

59

61

62

Villafontana

There's chemistry once the music gets going.

UABC medical campus

With their help, my grandfather's song will take form.

A house party in Calafia

Everyone will cheer.

He will be saved.

A bar by L. Montejano Road

We're still working on that song.

That annoying killer song.

65

67

68

Oh- NOW there's a crowd. Great.

75

78

82

91

By the way, Espinoza called. She wants to know when we'd want to use her studio.

Also, wanted to know what our idea for a band is.

What did she mean by that?

Do we have a long-term plan? That kind of thing.

Well, she's seen us at a couple of shows, and she's curious to know if we have a vision.

What did you tell her?

I said I'm my brother's guitarist who knows a little about recording. That you guys should talk to her.

Oh-Hiya, Beatriz.

94

97

108

116

118

What'd you
think?

125

131

141

143

144

146

147

Ready to write something right now?

157

158

159

163

164

(Reprise.)

171

191

SOMEWHERE IN 2004

The tunes that bring the smell of cement, sweat, and cheers.

Or make you feel alive in the unthinkable.

The ones that take us places...

THE GARAGE

BEATRIZ'S
BEDROOM

Beatriz   Abel   Diana   Ed   Fausto

AUTHOR'S NOTE

Suncatcher started simple: I wanted to make a comic about music, and I wanted a reason to draw instruments. Mostly guitars.

In the beginning of 2008, I didn't have a story. I had a few plot elements, but nothing specific. During a road trip, I committed to the idea of an enchanted guitar and the musician who would break that spell. I thought I could build something from that. I filled pages with concepts and themes rather than a story arc. It was an incoherent start, but eventually I had a beginning, middle, and end.

The script developed little by little until I found the story I wanted to tell. By talking to musicians and enthusiasts, the story was set in my hometown, Mexicali, during the music scene of the early 2000s. It turned into a story about songwriting, professional aspirations, and personal responsibilities. *Suncatcher* became about Beatriz and her relationships with other musicians.

It took more than seven years to discover all the characters. By 2015, I used my notes and interviews to put together a story that felt sincere. As I continued to show friends what I had, I listened to their advice. Every time I would get stuck, I'd turn to them, and sure enough, they would either reaffirm my choices or help me make better ones. Much like an album, this comic wouldn't have come together without the contributions of several talented artists.

I spent the last months of 2017 and the first half of 2018 producing *Suncatcher*. From pencils to digital lettering, the comic that started as an excuse to draw guitars turned into a dream project, set in a time and place where I developed my love for music. *Suncatcher* turned into my opportunity to show Mexicali to readers. It became a reminder that what makes it a wonderful place is its residents. It was my chance to talk about things I value.

Beatriz's journey is the most personal story I have written to date. I wish I could sum up *Suncatcher*'s over-a-decade-long voyage in a concise manner, but much like the process of putting this book together, I would leave a lot of things out. So I'll go with this: It has been a dream come true, and it couldn't have happened without the support and help of family, friends, and of course, Mexicali and music.

Thank you.

ACKNOWLEDGMENTS

Most special thank you to my family and friends, the whole family Pimienta and the whole family Garcia for their support and influence. Particularly my immediate family: Maria Eugenia, Fatima, Jose Mario, and Jose Maria Pimienta.

To my dearest ones: Vera, Tury, Chris, and Picha for letting me be in their band. Kristen Gish for all her support and feedback.

Mara, Chely, Carlos, David, Caro, Faister, Ana Bertha, Joss, Julie, Tony, Jessica, Colunga, Nayeli, Dany, Pamela, Rene, Chelsea, Mariana, Angelina, Andres, Argentina, Mario Vilchis, Anabel, Ema Karen, and Mare for being there during the making of this book and having a strong influence on the story I wanted to tell about the city where we grew up.

Whitney Leopard for believing in this book and helping me navigate the logistics of turning my idea into a reality. Her editorial input made all the difference. And thank you to Gina Gagliano and Patrick Crotty for helping to bring this story to life at RH Graphic.

Kel McDonald, Kara Leopard, Lisa Dosson, Francisco Guerrero, and Neleuz DG for being morally and artistically supportive. Rhiannon Rasmussen-Silverstein for all her prepress assistance and patience during the making of the Kickstarter edition of this book. Nate Peikos and Blambot for the fonts. Dan Downing for helping me with the video for the Kickstarter campaign and always being enthusiastic about making art. Tabula Rasa for lending a song to the Kickstarter campaign and for being influential musicians. El Dorado Printshop and Embroidery for their help in the Kickstarter campaign, and in particular to Beto Nes for all his art across Mexicali.

For their contribution with interviews about the Mexicali music scene, thank you to Neleuz, Rocio Chavez, Chely Mosqueda, Koko (Eduardo Rodriguez Baldas), Cholopunk Delinkuanxia (Ernesto Yañez Carrillo), Pablo Mérida, Skaren Martinez, Meggan Amos, Kristen Gish, Cecil Castellucci, Gera Montoya, and Angelina de Luca.

Some of the most inspiring local bands were Chelsea, Chapulines, Lencería, Requiem, Kinkinervia, Mexican Deal, Donnie Brasco, Uno Menos, Dulce Señor, Panic!, Madre Mostaza, In Site, Dulcinea, No Moral, Lusid, Cast, Tabula Rasa, Los Martes, Arsenal, Los García, Barra Brava, Ella Tiene Dos Androides, Letters from Readers, Todo Mal, Activistas Del Amor, Dead Stanleys, and a band my friends and I only heard once during a show that was being canceled as it was starting. They didn't introduce themselves, but as we were escorted out, we asked for their name and they just yelled "Cabeza de Monda," which we were pretty sure was fake. We never heard you again, but what we heard was *amazing*. I sincerely hope you're still making music.

Big and special thank you to my grandparents, Jose María Pimienta, Guadalupe Rendón, Mario Armando García, and Hortencia García. Their stories kept my imagination ignited.

A big thank you to all friends who contributed in one way or another, some via Kickstarter and others with a solid and encouraging cheer: Olivia, Ruth, Lulu, Tita, Martha, Diana, Nanda, Beto, Market, Raul Díaz, Hunter and Alice, Madison Carroll, Rosendo Cázares, Will, Amanda and J White, Lauren Stewart, Cari Jacobs, Guillermo Lizarraga, Luis Eduardo Oliver, Alejandro Espinoza, Van Jensen, Jarrett Williams, Tom Lyle, Andrea Bell, the Hornsby family, the Seidman family, Shawn Strider, Fernanda Martinez, Lisa, Roger, Carl, Abe and everyone at Model Drawing Collective, Kaitlyn and the Rosenberg family, Brian R., Talia Ellis, Drew, Melissa, Kari, Lauren, Corrine, Marissa Mozek, RJ, Paul, and every other Kickstarter backer.

THANK YOU. THANK YOU. THANK YOU.

NOTES

THROUGHOUT THE BOOK, THERE ARE EASTER EGGS REFERRING TO MEXICALI AND PUNK ROCK CULTURE.

PAGE 1: "And for this gift I feel blessed" from "Smells Like Teen Spirit" by Nirvana.

PAGE 3: Reference to Pink Floyd's *Pulse*, The Beatles' *Abbey Road* and *Yellow Submarine*, and Nirvana, Guns N' Roses, Metallica, Queen, Sonic Youth, Café Tacvba, Enanitos Verdes, Zurdok's "Luna" music video, La Ley, and Maldita Vecindad's *El Circo*.

PAGE 4: Reference to Resorte's "Aqui no es donde."

PAGE 5: Nirvana, Loga, Axel Rose, Café Tacvba, El Circo, Caifanes, Lexington Field, El Rosario Sinaloa, La Place Calafia. April 8, 1994, is an important day for grunge fans, as it was when Kurt Cobain was found dead at his Seattle home.

PAGE 6: Reference to Radiohead's *Kid A*.

PAGE 7: Cast is a Mexicali band.

PAGE 14: Canal 66 is a Mexicali television station.

PAGE 15: October 2, 1968, is remembered for the Tlatelolco tragedy in Mexico City. October 2, 1995, is when Oasis released *(What's the Story) Morning Glory?*

PAGE 16: Mexicali's Nuestra Señora de Guadalupe Cathedral.

PAGE 17: June 16, 1997, is when Radiohead's *OK Computer* was released.

PAGE 20: "On a Friday" is a Radiohead reference. "Florecita Rockera" is a song by the Colombian band Aterciopelados. Madre Mostaza was a Mexicali punk rock band.

PAGE 21: Boulevard Benito Juárez. "Eits" is a form of "Hey." "¿Quiúbole?" is a form of "What's up?"

PAGE 29: "Gimme tha Power" is a song from Molotov's debut album.

PAGE 32: Mazatlán is a city in the state of Sinaloa. El Sinaloense music sheet by Severiano Briseño.

PAGE 34: Silverchair's "Anthem for the Year 2000." María Sabina shirt. 7500 1476 is the barcode for Cigarros delicados.

PAGE 35: Zurdok's third album, *Maquillaje*, was released on June 7, 2001. Logo on shirt is a reference to the band Jumbo.

PAGE 37: Ed wears a Pegamentos Industriales Galileo shirt. It's an industrial glue company in Mexicali.

PAGE 42: Boulevard Lázaro Cárdenas and its monument.

PAGE 43: The Fender Telecaster is similar to the one used in the 1986 film *Crossroads*. The poster references Águilas de Mexicali, a local baseball team.

PAGE 44: "En el Mero—Mero Calor" means "the very, very heavy heat." 91X radio station poster.

PAGE 46: La Abeja is a convenience store in Mexicali. Cheve is slang for beer.

PAGE 47: Arsenal, Panic, and Donnie Brasco are Mexicali bands. CBTIS is a Mexicali technical school. The Hecho en Mexico symbol is altered to say Hecho en Mexicali.

PAGE 48: Rococo Graves is a reference to Mexico City's punk rock band Panteon Rococo.

PAGE 50: Six is a convenience-store chain. DADGBE is a type of guitar tuning. La Chelsea is a Mexicali punk ska band.

PAGE 51: Lyrics to "Amor Instantáneo Ramen" by La Chelsea.

PAGE 56: Reference to Monumento de los Pioneros.

PAGE 57: "Punk rock, mi vida está bien" is the slogan of Mexicali band La Chelsea. Abel wears a Thrice *Identity Crisis* shirt. Ed wears a Weezer shirt. Diane wears a Héroes del Silencio shirt.

PAGE 59: "Corn chips gorros" is a reference to the corn chip brand Rancheritos. El Tri is a Mexican rock band.

PAGE 61: Beatriz is eating churros locos, a popular snack.

PAGE 64: Villafontana and Calafia are Mexicali neighborhoods. UABC is Baja California's state college. L. Montejano Road is a street.

PAGE 65: Diana wears a Caifanes shirt. Caifanes is a popular Mexican rock group.

PAGE 66: Beatriz and Abel's conversation is a reference to the song "The Man Who Sold the World" by David Bowie and covered by Nirvana.

PAGE 75: The posters in Beatriz's room make reference to many bands and to Mexicali's children's museum, Sol del Niño.

PAGE 78: Beatriz wears a shirt in reference to Guns N' Roses's *Appetite for Destruction* album.

PAGE 83: A view of Mexicali's civic center, movie theater, UABC Medicine's facility, Comercial Mexicana department store, Plaza Fiesta mall, and the bullfighting arena also used as a concert venue.

PAGE 85: Odisea 2002 was the name of Jumbo and Zurdok's national tour together in 2002.

PAGE 94: Ed eats carnitas rojas, which is a common dish in Mexicali Chinese food.

PAGE 96: Lenceria was a Mexicali rock band.

PAGE 110: Fiestas del Sol is the city fair.

PAGE 111: Beethoven's Ninth Symphony "Ode to Joy."

NOTES (CONTINUED)

PAGE 115: "No te dejes caer" is a song by Mexicali punk rock band Arsenal.

PAGE 122: Proconsa is a hardware store. "Morra" is slang for a girl. "Naco" is slang and a derogatory term for someone of low class or someone who behaves in an unruly manner. Beatriz wears a Felix the Cat shirt.

PAGE 135: At a Fiestas del Sol event. "Volcano's nerve" is a reference to Caifanes's album *El Nervio del Volcán.*

PAGE 146: "Wednesday (2 x 1)" is a reference to a policy in Mexicali movie theaters when tickets are half off every Wednesday.

PAGE 153: "Blistered hands" is a reference to the song "El Cachanilla." Beatriz wears a Requiem band shirt. Pemex is the name of the Mexican petrol company.

PAGE 154: Reference to Marshall Amps. A reference to Zurdok's "Luna" music video.

PAGE 157: The building number refers to Daft Punk's film *Interstella 5555.*

PAGE 195: Abel wear a Trio shirt.

PAGE 197: La Ley's album *Invisible.* Oasis's *(What's the Story) Morning Glory?* Rage Against the Machine poster.

PAGE 198: They pass by Mexicali landmarks: the old Brewery, the Vicente Guerrero monument, and Mariachi Plaza.

PAGE 201: A framed image of Mexicali's Chinesca monument, which celebrates the sisterhood between Mexicali and China.

PAGE 204: UABC's Engineering campus.

PAGE 205: El Centinela is the name of Mexicali's mountain.

PAGE 206: Vive Latino 2004 poster.

SKETCHES

MEXICALI: CREST AND GEOGRAPHY

The Mexicali crest was designed in 1968 by Sergio Ocampo Ramirez. It was chosen by Municipal President Jose Maria Rodriguez Merida on April 9, 1968.

Meanings behind the crest design:

The red strip represents the Colorado River.

The blue represents the waters of the Gulf of California.

The ocher is the desert.

The cotton bud represents the fields of cotton in the valleys.

The mountain is El Centinela, a natural boundary between the United States and Mexico and a traveler's guide.

The gear with the atom represents Mexicali's science and industrial developments.

Slogan: Tierra Calida, which means Warm Land, a reference to both the region's weather and its reputation for warmhearted people.

Name: Mexi/Cali, which comes from a combination of Mexico and California.

The red sun references the region's weather.

The eagle is a reference to the Aztec eagle, symbolizing the origins of some of its population.

Jose Pimienta grew up in Mexicali and studied sequential art at the Savannah College of Art and Design. He now lives in Los Angeles, making comics and storyboards. He still loves discovering music.

@joepi
@thejoepi
@joepiworks
josepimienta.com

RH GRAPHIC

THE SUMMER 2020 LIST

CRABAPPLE TROUBLE
By Kaeti Vandorn

Life isn't easy when you're an apple.

Callaway and Thistle must figure out how to work together—with delicious and magical results.

Young Chapter Book

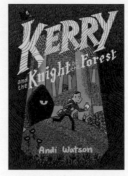

KERRY AND THE KNIGHT OF THE FOREST
By Andi Watson

Kerry needs to get home!

To get back to his parents, Kerry gets lost in a shortcut. He will have to make tough choices and figure out who to trust—or remain lost in the forest . . . forever.

Middle Grade

STEPPING STONES
By Lucy Knisley

Jen did not want to leave the city.

She did not want to move to a farm.

And Jen definitely did not want to get two new "sisters."

Middle Grade

SUNCATCHER
By Jose Pimienta

Beatriz loves music—more than her school, more than her friends—and she won't let anything stop her from achieving her dreams.

Even if it means losing everything else.

Young Adult

FIND US ONLINE AT @RHKIDSGRAPHIC AND RHKIDSGRAPHIC.COM